A Marriage
CAROL

A Marriage
CAROL

CHRIS FABRY &
GARY CHAPMAN

MOODY PUBLISHERS
CHICAGO

Edited by Elizabeth Cody Newenhuyse
Cover design: Julia Ryan / DesignByJulia.com
Interior design: Smartt Guys design
Cover images: Red door with wreath—iStockphoto.com / MPPHOTOInc.;
            Diamond Ring—iStockPhoto.com / Zentilia
Gary Chapman photo: Mike Apple
Chris Fabry photo: Herb Wetzel

Fabry, Chris, 1961-
The marriage carol / Chris Fabry and Gary Chapman.
    p. cm.
ISBN 978-0-8024-0264-6
1. Marriage--Fiction. 2. Christmas stories. I. Chapman, Gary D.
II. Title.
PS3556.A26M37 2011
813'.54--dc22

                    2011019289

We hope you enjoy this book from River North Fiction by Moody Publishers. Our goal is to provide high-quality, thought-provoking books and products that connect truth to your real needs and challenges. For more information on other books and products written and produced from a biblical perspective, go to www.moodypublishers.com or write to:

River North Fiction
Division of Moody Publishers
820 N. LaSalle Boulevard
Chicago, IL 60610

1 3 5 7 9 10 8 6 4 2

Printed in the United States of America

For the wounded, cold, and all who struggle.
May this story bring warmth, life, and above all, hope.

Prelude

I know what you will say. You married the wrong person.

I know because it is what I said. But that was before the winter of our discontent and the plans we made that Christmas Eve. That was before the snow.

The snow taught me something. It always teaches if you will let it. I learned it is a dangerous thing to have your eyes opened. It is dangerous to see. It is dangerous to love.

If we had simply *liked* each other so long ago, if we had only been searching for "happiness," things would be easier. When you are concerned only about feeling better you can move on, pick up your luggage, step off the train, and keep looking. But love makes you vulnerable to the cold. Love beckons you outside in a snowstorm, in a shaking, wobbling globe where there is no control, where you stand naked in bitter wind searching for what has been covered.

You cannot plan for love. You cannot choose against it once it has come. True love doesn't end once another steps away. You may forsake a person, a family, some location of the heart, but scars and memories cannot be discarded like used clothing. Love, if it is real, cannot be abandoned, because it does not come from yourself, but from an unseen spring. That Source provides nourishment and moisture for the soul.

Of course you will say that you never possessed true love. It was wrong at the start. Or that your love has frozen over time. Even if love is rock-hard, it cannot be killed, the waters cannot be held back. Love will always find its own way, even if the droplets have turned to ice.

Here's what I know. Our lives are bound by our choices, and our choices are like snowflakes that pile around us until the warmth we felt inside grows dormant, withers, and dies. Then we are left to ourselves and the consequences. The heart is drawn to the warmth of spring and sun and life. With love, we move purposefully and intuitively. Without it, we stumble, blindly searching for the narrow path.

I will tell you what happened. Though painful, I will show you the truth. I pray you will listen. I pray you will open up some small part of you, a sliver of that good heart, a glimmer of your eye, something in your gut that is telling you this is the way, this is the path through the drifting and piling in your life. There must be some part of you that believes in miracles; that death, though it feels like it, is not the end. That what has been sealed in a tomb might rise once again.

I used to dream of love as if it were a memory. I used to touch the mirror and wipe away steam to see my reflection, clouded and blurry. I longed for a clear vista of life. That is what I was given. What I saw in myself was an arid, desert wasteland.

There is no barren place on earth that love cannot grow a garden. Not even your heart.

The Shortcut

"When do we tell the children?"

He said it without feeling, without emotion, without giving weight to the words. He said it as though he was asking the latest stock price for Microsoft or Google. These were his first words after nearly twenty minutes in the car together. On our anniversary.

"After Christmas," I said, matching his evenness, his coldness. "Not tonight or tomorrow."

"Don't you think they know by now? At least that something's up?"

"Not David, he's too young. Justin asks questions and just looks at me with those doe eyes, but he keeps it in. Becca is the one I worry about."

"Kids are resilient. If they don't know, they'll understand. It's for the best. For all of us."

I hope he's right.

"Now they'll have two Christmases," he said.

The windshield wipers beat their own rhythm as wet snow fell like rain. The landscape had retreated under the white covering, adding to a previous snowfall that hadn't fully melted. The roadway, where you could see it, shone black with treachery from the moisture and falling temperatures. Cars inched along ahead of us on an incline as Jacob drove faster, crowding the car in front of us, looking for a chance to pass.

"Are you sure he'll be at his office?" I said, looking out the window, bracing for impact. "In this weather? On Christmas Eve?"

"He's still there. I called before we left. The papers are ready."

"Does he have a family?" I said.

"What?" He said it with a healthy dose of condescension, and added a look I couldn't stand. The look I could live the rest of my life without seeing.

"Does he have a family. A wife? Kids?"

"I have no idea." More condescension. "I didn't know

that was a prerequisite for you."

"It's not. I was just wondering. Working on Christmas Eve. No wonder he's a divorce lawyer."

So much for a congenial discussion. The silence was getting to him now and he flipped on a talk station. I was surprised he hadn't done that earlier. The clock showed 3:18, and a delayed Rush Limbaugh was going into a break. A commercial about an adjustable bed. Local traffic and the forecast. Snarled intersections and cold weather reporting. Expect an even whiter Christmas. Several inches whiter. Maybe more. A cold front moving in and more precipitation at higher elevations.

"Can we listen to something else?" I said.

He suppressed a huff and pressed the FM button. This was his car so nothing on the FM dial was pre-set. He hit "scan."

He frowned. "Punch it when you hear something you like."

I passed on Gene Autry and Rudolph. The song brought an ache for the children. Especially David who still believed in Santa and reindeer. At the next station, José Feliciano was down to his last *Feliz Navidad*. On the left side of the dial, the local Christian station played yet another version of "Silent Night." I couldn't stay there because of the guilt of what we were doing.

Paul McCartney said the mood was right and the spirit was up and he was simply having a wonderful Christmastime. I wished I could say the same. The band Journey sang "Don't Stop Believin'," but I had stopped long ago, at least concerning our marriage. This was not how we planned it twenty years ago, though the snowstorm felt similar. Twenty Christmas Eves after I walked the aisle in a dress my mother and I had picked out, I was wearing jeans, an old T-shirt, and an overcoat, cruising in sneakers down the slippery road to a no-fault divorce.

Three children and the bird would live with me (a dog made too much mess and Jacob is allergic to cats), and he would move into an apartment after the New Year. Jacob promised to stay involved. There wasn't another woman, as far as I knew, as far as he would let on. That wasn't our problem. The problems were much deeper than infidelity.

I hit the button on singer Imogen Heap. Nothing at all about Christmas. Just quirky music and a synthesized voice that took my mind off the present, which is supposed to be a gift, I know. I've heard that.

"I'm done with this road," Jacob said. "I'm taking the shortcut."

"Over the hill? In this weather?" Two interrogatives to his one statement of fact.

"It'll cut the travel in half. Nobody takes County Line anymore."

"Don't you think we should stay where they've plowed?"

He ignored my entreaty and turned left sharply. The rear of the car slid to the right. I grabbed the door handle instinctively as he corrected. He gave the Jacob head shake, and with shake you get eye roll and a sigh on the side.

"Trust me for once, will you?" he said.

I wanted to bring up a million little ways I've tried to trust him. A million little ways I've been let down. For twenty years I've searched for reasons to place my trust squarely on his shoulders. But how do you trust someone who has failed at the life you wanted? There were flashes of caring, a dozen roses to say "I'm sorry," but the roses wilted and died. And then we started on this direction, him on the Interstate and me on the Frontage Road, separate but still traveling in a semblance of the same direction. Two moons orbiting the same planet, rarely intersecting.

"I don't want the kids going to our funeral," I muttered.

He slammed on the brakes and I yelped as we went into another slide. Passive-aggressive driving is his specialty.

"Fine, I'll turn around."

Both hands to my head, tears welling, I hit the power button on the radio and heard myself say, "No, just keep going."

County Line Road used to be one of my favorite drives. In summer when the hills were in full bloom and Becca was little, I would take the shortcut over the mountain to show her how other people lived—not jammed into houses so close you couldn't breathe, but on long, flowering acres with roaming cows, horses enjoying fresh pasture, and people living less like hamsters on wheels and more close to the earth. As a child, I dreamed of living on a horse farm, riding them every day, cleaning stalls, feeding them oats and apples. But those dreams died a slow death, four hooves sticking out of the frozen snow, along with the dream about a happy family, a good marriage, fulfillment, purpose, and a lifelong love.

Jacob flicked on the radio as we ascended, obviously disturbed by silence again. Santa sightings by the chief meteorologist gave way to a nine-car pileup and a shut-down on the Interstate.

"Told you it was smart to take County Line," he said. I wouldn't call it smug. Jacob wasn't capable of smug. He was more a river of indifference. Perhaps that was it. He was the river, I was the highway. The passion was gone. Was it ever there? It's hard to remember a fire when the embers are covered with snow. Yes, it existed at one point, but then so did dinosaurs.

We had been advised that it was better for us to decide on the distribution of our assets—the house, the cars, and the kids—before we went to court. The attorney would represent me, since he couldn't represent us both, but we had amicably decided the allocation of everything down to the bird and our cell phones because said lawyer told us once the court got involved in deciding who gets the wagon-wheel coffee table and what visitation rights will be, things go south quickly and the children are the ones who suffer.

"Don't give control of the future of your family to a judge," the lawyer said in our last consult. "A judge doesn't want to be the parent. He or she wants you to work out a plan that's best for the kids. Do this now and you won't have to go through that pain in a courtroom. You don't want a judge choosing who gets how much time with the kids."

We were doing what was best. We were being grown-ups, trying to absorb the pain of our choices and the changes that had made us such different people. We were sparing our offspring more pain, blocking access to the horror show that was our marriage. We were miles apart at the same dinner table, in a bitter relational chill, skating on precariously thin ice. And this was our effort to do the responsible thing; pull the family off before the surface cracked beneath us. We were also saving Jacob a ton of money, which is what he really cared about. If he could have purchased a divorce at Walmart, he would have. And he would have used a coupon.

"Remind you of anything?" Jacob said, his voice snapping me back to reality.

"The commercial?"

"No, the snow. Remind you of anything in the past?"

"Just like our honeymoon," I said indifferently.

"You didn't trust my driving then, either."

"I wasn't worried about your driving."

"What's that supposed to mean?"

Heavy sigh. "Nothing. I was scared that night."

"Scared? Of me?"

"Scared about what we had just done. That it wouldn't last. That I wouldn't be the wife you wanted."

"Or that I wouldn't be the man you wanted. Guess those fears turned into reality," he said, sticking the fork in the overdone turkey.

"Yeah. It just took longer than I expected." I spoke staring out the window at the early December darkness. Clouds blocked the sun and hung over us like specters, spilling wet tears from heaven's portals. Higher we climbed, into the unincorporated, untarnished mountainside. Long stretches of pasture and woods stared back at me.

He shook his head and dipped the volume on the radio only a little. "If it makes any difference, I'm sorry it turned out this way."

Out of the blue, it almost sounded sincere. I turned and found him looking at me. We were children when we were married, which was part of the problem. "I do," had turned into famous last words. His hair, once thick and buoyant, had grayed and receded in a forced march by the unrelenting taskmaster of time. He had refused to wear contacts, preferring the same style of glasses that had gone out of fashion and returned like my favorite pumps. Crow's-feet around his eyes, and rosy, youthful cheeks that had turned puffy and wan. An objective viewer would say he was still handsome in some cherubic way. But I am not an objective viewer. Not that his slight weight gain made any difference to me. I always thought he was handsome.

"Your sister called before we left," he said, switching the subject during my pregnant pause. "I told her you'd get back with her."

My sister. The Christian mother. Loving, kind, a sweetness you could make a Blizzard with at Dairy Queen. And yet, unapproachable. As much as she said she did, she couldn't understand our problems. And wouldn't you know it, she had to confide in our parents and let them know our marriage was on shaky ground.

He stared at me, but I couldn't look him in the eye. "I'll call her after we sign the papers."

His eyes were too much. Too blue. Nearly opaque. That was the first thing I remembered about him. Those eyes—almost penetrating the soul, it seemed.

When I looked up we were nearing a curve, and through the haze and blowing snow I noticed two headlights bearing down on us like our oncoming future. I couldn't scream, couldn't speak, just threw out a hand and pointed.

Instinct. His foot to the pedal. Steering wheel one way, then the other. Fishtailing. A truck's air horn. Jacob reached out for me.

Spinning.

Weightless.

Out of control.

A snow globe shaken and dropped.

Alone

I awoke, cold and alone, the keys still swaying in the ignition. Acrid smoke filled the car — the air bags had deployed and were now limp soldiers. The windshield was smashed and the windows around me were frost covered. It felt like a vehicular igloo. I rubbed a hand over the ice on the window but had to scrape with a fingernail to see. There was nothing but piled snow outside, and the door wouldn't budge.

I climbed over to the driver's side and opened the door. The warning bell weakly alerted me that the key was still in the ignition.

"Jacob?"

Nothing but the sound of wet snow falling. The car

had come to rest in a snowbank, pushed into a clump of thin birch trees growing by the curve, but there was no sign of my husband. I looked for tracks on his side of the car but there were none.

I pulled my feet inside, closed the door, and felt my head. No significant bumps. I pulled the rearview mirror down to see if I had ruptured a major artery but the mirror came off in my hand. No blood, but the mirror showed lines and wrinkles I hadn't noticed. Thanks to Clairol, my hair had maintained a deep auburn. Brown eyes that looked tired and empty. No makeup, not even lipstick. If I had worn a head covering I could be on the cover of an Amish tragedy.

I turned the key and the engine sputtered, coughed, and sneezed, but didn't start. My breath became a fog when I exhaled, and my hands were quickly turning to ice. I opened the door again and yelled for my husband. Nothing but the echo of my voice and the *tick*, *tick* of ice and snow descending.

I dug into my purse and pulled out my cell phone. I could tell the kids we'd been in an accident and then I'd call 911. There was no reception in the area. No bars on the phone.

That was where Jacob went, to find a place to call 911. *But why would he leave without telling me?*

My teeth chattered, and every time I shoved my hands into the overcoat they felt colder. The cloud cover blocked the sun but gave enough light to see the landscape. Through the intensifying snow were rolling hills and trees, dense wooded areas as well as pasture with several inches of covering and in some places a few feet of snow where the wind had fiercely blown.

I took the keys and set out on foot, looking around the curve and down the hill for the tractor trailer. The road under the top layer of snow was an ice rink, and I lamented not wearing hiking boots. Maybe Jacob had followed the truck, trying to aid the driver who had no doubt plunged into the abyss. As I rounded the curve below our spinout, I expected to see flashers in the fog, the contents of the trailer spilled on the road or the hillside below, but everything was clear. There were no skid marks, other than ours. No gaping hole in the barbed wire fence. No deceased driver.

"Jacob!" I yelled, my voice echoing off the wet hillsides and trees. The only thing worse than hearing my husband's voice was not hearing my husband's voice.

My cell phone still had no signal, and the battery was low. Darkness was coming quickly and the cold moved from my fingers and toes inward and upward. The only footprints leading from the car were my own and I followed them back. We had spun a 360 and another 180 into the snowbank against the trees. Other than the deployed airbags and windshield, there didn't seem to be more damage, but I wasn't worried about the car at that point.

Through the trees and snow I spotted a glimmer of light, a faint glow on the hillside. If it was a house, there had to be a road, but a quick look at the winding road that wound upward and away from the house led me to believe the fastest route was on foot across the pasture and up the hillside. Perhaps Jacob had gone there to get help.

I slung my purse over my shoulder and started down the hill, gaining unintended momentum and stopping myself by grabbing a fence post. I climbed through the barbed wire and a few steps later tripped on something and fell, the contents of my purse spilling into the snow. My face, my hands, my legs were now wet and stinging, the wind biting. I located my wallet, phone, and keys and left the rest. I zipped the coat as far as it would go and set off through the pasture. Snow snuck into my shoes, and my ankles and shins were the next victims. What I wouldn't give for a fresh pair of Jacob's unstylish tube socks I berated him for wearing.

When I hit the hillside, I lost sight of the glow. Dead leaves and dry branches cracked and hissed underneath the layers of snow. An eerie darkness enveloped me, and I wished I had a flashlight. Why hadn't I stayed on the road? If it wasn't for the little trees that gave me leverage to pull myself higher, I might have given up.

"Jacob?"

An enormous crow landed in a tree above me and cawed, daring me to continue. I was too exhausted to snap off a tree limb and throw it at him and too cold to make a snowball. He cawed again as I grabbed the tree and pulled myself forward and then awkwardly took to his wings and flew across the white meadow, dipping and wobbling until he thumped onto an old stump. That's when I saw the car on the road, headlights scanning the hillside as they passed the curve, not even slowing at our spinout. If I had stayed I could have flagged them down. I'd be warm. Or maybe in a car with a serial killer.

Where is your husband when you need him? I never went for the strong, silent type, or the macho male/weekend warrior, but I would have taken a gun-toting, beer-guzzling squirrel hunter right then—to swoop me up and carry me the rest of the way.

The cold and wetness stung my face, and so did the briars I crashed through near the top of the hill. I wiped something wet away from the scratches and tears filled my eyes. My nose was dripping, my lips were numb, and my hair wet with melting snow that had fallen from the trees. My thighs, not the highlight of my anatomy, burned from the long pull uphill, but were also chilled and frozen. I was glad I didn't have a mirror right then, because I would have needed counseling to shake the indelible image.

At the top of the hill I saw the warm glow of the house in the distance. Feet frozen, I moved through a tall drift toward the yellow light. My face was so cold I was afraid my skin would crack if I opened my mouth to call out, so I just put one foot in front of the other. I navigated the backyard slowly, aided only by the light from the back windows. There was a child's swing set I didn't see that caused a problem for my forehead and a trestle I navigated around, but I finally made it to the side of the house and around a shoveled but ice-covered walkway.

A lamp near the driveway gave enough light for me to find the wraparound porch. It was a two-story home, wide and tall, with one light on upstairs. In the front window stood a Christmas tree with sparkling white lights that could have been featured on the cover of *Better Homes and Gardens*. The six-panel front door was painted a deep red, with a door knocker in the shape of an engagement ring—or so it seemed to me. Above the knocker was a beautiful wreath fashioned from evergreens and mistletoe. If I hadn't been so cold I would have admired it longer, but I reached out a frigid hand to the knocker. As I did, the curtain inside, which covered the small windows beside the door, moved slightly, and a tiny dog pressed its nose to the glass and barked.

The sound of heavy footsteps on hardwood. The door opened and an older man stood there, reaching to gather me into the warmth of the room. He was tall and heavyset, and looked like some actor who always gets picked for the part of the president or angry police sergeant who's frustrated with his officers. He carried an afghan and swept it over my shoulders with one quick throw and pulled it tight around me.

"You're freezing," he said, closing the door and getting on one knee before me. "Let's take those shoes off and get you over by the fire." He took off my shoes and slipped my dripping wet socks from my feet. I looked down on his bald spot, the gray hair forming a perfect *O* at the top of his head.

"What were you doing out there?"

"There was an accident," I said, teeth chattering. "I can't find my husband. He didn't come here, did he?"

"We haven't had any visitors with the storm. What type of accident?"

I explained and he listened intently, putting my shoes and socks over the heating vent. He stood with some effort, his knees cracking, and looked at the scratches on my face.

"I suspect he went to look for help or a cell signal, like you suggest," he said. "He's probably worried about you."

If he was so worried, why would he abandon me?

Water dripped from my hair onto the shiny wood

floor. I tried to stay on the welcome mat so as not to leak all over the entry. His face seemed warm and kind.

"Don't worry about the snow. It's just water, after all. Now come on over to the fire. We'll get you warm and cozy."

I slipped on the wet floor and he took my arm and guided me to the living room. He walked with a noticeable limp and when we reached an overstuffed, leather chair, he turned it toward the fireplace. Three huge logs burned and crackled, and their warmth and aroma gave me a fresh vision of welcome that covered me as well as the afghan.

He sat me down and pulled a footstool close, then draped a blanket from one of the couches over my legs and feet. "I'll be right back with something to warm you up on the inside." He left and the little dog returned, a teacup Yorkshire terrier that sniffed at my shoes and socks, then padded toward the chair, its ears up and eyes searching my face, as if it understood pain.

"Hey little guy," I said, reaching out a hand. He was reticent at first, backing up. He licked his nose and yawned, then crept closer as I held out my hand. He sniffed at it and sat again, looking into my soul, into all the hurt and coldness. Something about that dog caused the tears to well up inside me, something I didn't understand, couldn't understand. Jacob said dogs cause too much trouble. Too much mess. He couldn't stand hair on the furniture and the scratches on the floor and doors.

"I see you've met Rue," the man said when he returned with a towel. I dried my hair and kept the towel on my shoulders for any stray droplets. He also brought some woolen socks and I slipped them on.

"He's gorgeous," I said. "Such a wonderful color and shine to his coat. And a sweet disposition."

He patted my blanket and Rue jumped up on my lap and sat, wiggling his stubby tail and arching his back into me like we had known each other forever. I laughed at the feeling of something so pure and innocent excited to sit with me. He licked at my hands, then settled into a curl on my thighs and put his head toward the fire, content.

"Do you mind if I use your phone to call my children?" I said.

He gave a pained look and retrieved a handset from an end table. He clicked it on and listened. "The phone's been out all afternoon. Probably ice on the lines. And the cell phone reception is almost nonexistent up here."

"What about your computer? I could send—"

He chuckled. "Sorry, ma'am. We don't have access to that either. Decided a long time ago to cut that from the budget. But I'll go right out and look for your husband."

"His name is Jacob. And I'm Marlee Ebenezer. Thank you for taking me in like this."

The teakettle whistled from the kitchen. "I'll be right back," he said.

I stroked the dog's fur and looked around the room. Other than my leather chair, two other couches and a loveseat were arranged around the fireplace. On the mantel was a simple wreath and below it, a snow globe with a cross inside. Bookshelves flanked the fireplace. It was all I could do not to get up and examine the hundreds of volumes there, but I was too content and too warm with Rue on my lap. There were pictures, as well, of smiling couples standing together, posing for the camera. Most of the pictures were taken in front of the fireplace or in the backyard by the lattice.

A coffee table held a single candle, a Bible, and a purple book underneath. On the hearth were fireplace utensils—a poker, shovel, tongs, and broom. Beside it was a long-handled pot with two other smaller pots inside with the same size handles. They were gold and looked barely used.

The fire popped, and Rue gave a head-jerk and then settled again. The screen kept any stray embers from flying.

The tree made quite an impression at the bay window, but there was something strange about the room, something I couldn't pinpoint. Then it hit me that it was what *wasn't* in the room: a television. There was no sign of one.

"I have some three-bean chili cooking," the man said as he returned. "It'll be ready in a little bit. This should be a good start."

He shakily handed me a mug and saucer. The tea bag tag hung over the side and I recognized the familiar colors of my favorite tea.

"It's Ginger Lemon with just a drop or two of honey," the man said.

"Just the way I like it. Thank you."

The mug spread warmth to my whole body, and Rue sniffed at the saucer when I placed it on the arm of the chair.

"What are those pots?" I said.

He paused a moment, searching for the words. "Family heirloom. I'll tell you about them when I get back. Let the tea warm you, and I'll get your chili after I find your husband."

"This is very kind of you. Thank you."

He smiled at me as he put on his coat and hat and disappeared into the garage. The smell of the tea brought back memories, ones I didn't want to dredge up. Fights with Jacob; arguments and outbursts from me and the silence of a man resigned to something other than love. I hated associating those memories with the tea, but some things you can't control.

My mind raced through the possibilities of what had happened on the road. Sure, Jacob could have gone off on his own, looking for help, but what if someone wasn't paying attention while they drove along? What if someone had skidded into him somewhere up the road? Or perhaps the truck driver had taken him for help.

Something creaked above and Rue's body tensed, his ears pricked. In a flash he was off my lap and up the stairs, his little legs churning. He disappeared at the top of the stairs and his nails clicked over the hardwood.

The old man returned and hung his coat and hat on the hall tree. "I found your car, but there's no sign of Jacob. Checked with the neighbors, too. It's nasty on the roads. Almost got stuck even though I have four-wheel drive." He picked up the phone but it was still dead. "Maybe he got a ride down the hill. I left a note on the front seat telling him where you are. Put the emergency flashers on, too, but that battery is pretty weak."

"I suppose that's all we can do now," I said.

"Other than pray," he said.

I nodded. "I suppose there is that."

He disappeared into the kitchen and returned with a steaming bowl of chili with cornbread that tasted so sweet it melted in my mouth. He headed upstairs with another bowl and Rue met him at the top, wagging his tail and dancing on the hardwood like a trained circus animal.

I had finished my bowl when he returned and he offered me another, but I was content. He pulled a chair beside me and settled in, cradling his own bowl and warming both hands with it.

"Who else is here?" I said.

"Excuse me?"

"You said, 'we' when I first arrived. That 'we' haven't had any visitors. And I heard noise while you were gone."

"No one is here but my wife and me. She's resting upstairs."

"Is something wrong with her?"

"Nothing time and life haven't done." He paused and there seemed to be a bit of sadness in it. "And what brought you out to these parts?"

I told him we were on our way to an attorney's office to sign divorce papers. No sense beating around the bush. I let that sink in and expected some kind of apology for prying, but he didn't seem shocked.

"Have you been planning this long?" he said.

I told him more about us. More than I wanted, but it just seemed to spill out. And he didn't stop me.

"That's a lot of years to be married. What's the main reason? Has Jacob abused you in some way?"

"No, there's no abuse."

"Is there another woman?"

"I don't think so. His other woman is his work."

"Have you tried counseling?"

I nodded. "A few times. A pastor once. A psychologist. Went to a marriage seminar one weekend a few years ago."

He reached toward the coffee table. "Have you tried—"

"The books? Let me tell you about the books I've read. Stacked on my nightstand. I listened to them on CD in the carpool lane. Don't give me another book. I've tried everything. Even called a radio program once asking for advice. Nothing works. We're just not right for each other."

"But you were, at one point?"

"In the beginning, sure. Anyone can stay in love at the beginning, I think. But through the years, and with the kids, we just grew apart. He threw himself into his work and hobbies, and my heart turned toward the children."

"And here you are twenty years later, strangers."

"Exactly."

"Tell me about your children. How old are they?"

As he crumbled his cornbread into his chili, I told him everything. All the way down to what David said in the bathroom while he was sitting, studying the patterns in the tile. The man laughed with me and shook his head like it was his own grandchild.

"You mentioned a pastor," he said as he finished his chili and placed the bowl on the coffee table. "What about your spiritual life?"

I laughed, though it wasn't funny, and stared at the fire. "I know it's not true, but it almost feels like I don't have any right to talk to God."

"Why would you say that?"

"Because I know it's a sin to get a divorce. That's how I was raised. And once God is ticked off at you, He won't listen to your prayers."

"Well, it's true that God hates divorce. But that doesn't mean you shouldn't talk with Him. He's a forgiving God. And part of the reason He hates divorce is the pain and heartache it creates in the people He loves."

"You sound like a pastor."

He smiled. "I guess in a way I am. You came across the field, didn't you? You didn't see the sign in front."

"What sign? I couldn't see ten feet in front of my face."

"Years ago this place was a funeral home. Didn't get much business way out here, so they sold it. We turned it into a retreat center. For struggling couples. People who've given up or those who just want to grow closer." He pointed at the pictures in the bookshelf. "Some of our graduates."

I couldn't hold back the laughter. "That has to be the definition of irony. I take shelter at a marriage retreat that used to be a funeral home."

"I don't think it's by chance that you're here." He spoke with an edge of certainty.

"You saved all of those marriages?"

"Not me. And sadly, not all of them were saved. People make their own choices. We can't control what anyone does, but we can be there to walk with them. Many were right on the brink, like you. From where I sit, I'd say you were allowed this divine appointment for a purpose."

"Or maybe that eighteen-wheeler was God's way of punishing us for what we were about to do."

"I prefer to think of it as a wake-up call. It's never too late to do something good for your marriage."

I shook my head. "We've made up our minds. There's no hope left."

He folded his wrinkled hands and looked at the pictures. "I've heard that a few times over the years. And I'd like to suggest something about hope. Why don't you and your husband hold on to the hope I have for you?"

"A man we can't even find?"

"A man who probably doesn't want to go through with this any more than you."

"How can you say that? You don't even know him. You don't know me."

He pursed his lips. "I'm going on experience. Most people don't want to throw away their marriage. Working together for twenty years and giving a lot of money to lawyers doesn't make sense."

"You're right about that. The lawyer Jacob found is cut-rate. The only reason he would stay with me is if he could save money, not because of love."

"So you're going through with the divorce even though you know it's not the answer. You just don't see another way out."

Though I wanted to change the subject, I couldn't. The old man had nailed my inner feelings. His questions led me further toward the hurt and betrayal I felt at my husband for not *seeing* me. Not noticing all I did to make our lives work. Of course Jacob felt the same way, that I had not fully engaged in the relationship for some time. That I had given up, disengaged. That my mind was elsewhere, even during lovemaking. Which was true.

"I know I'm not happy where I am," I said. "And neither is he. Isn't that what marriage is supposed to be? We're supposed to love each other. We're supposed to complete each other. Isn't there a verse that says God wants us to be happy?"

He rubbed the stubble on his chin. "There's a verse that says Jesus came to give life and give it abundantly. But God doesn't exist to make you and me happy. Some of the most committed followers of God I've ever met have been in miserable circumstances."

"Good thing you're not a pastor, because that kind of message wouldn't exactly fill pews or the offering plate."

He smiled. "True. But notice I said their circumstances were miserable. But they were content in their situation. They saw that God was working in them and through them in spite of what was happening on the outside."

"Well, I don't think God's at work with us. He abandoned our marriage a long time ago. I'm just following Him out the door."

"Are you *sure* He's abandoned you?"

"What do you mean? You think God's been working?"

"Maybe God has been closer than you know. Even

bringing you here suggests to me that there's still hope."

"I don't know how many ways I can say it. *It's over.* He's picked out his apartment. I get the house and van and we share custody of the kids. Twenty years ago tonight we started this journey and it's about to end."

The man's tired eyes lit up. "Tonight's your anniversary?"

"Yes. In a snowstorm. We thought it would be romantic to have a Christmas Eve wedding. What were we thinking? We haven't been able to celebrate our anniversary since our kids were born. Not that we would celebrate now."

He stood and walked toward the fireplace. "Interesting. Twenty years ago tonight something pivotal happened. Something that changed your life. Twenty years later on the exact same date you're making another pivotal choice."

"It's just a day on the calendar."

"I'm not so sure. Dates are important. And there's meaning behind a heavy snowfall. There's power in it."

"You're losing me, here. What do you mean?"

"You've seen fake snow in movies. You can tell it every time you see it. The stuff blows around. Won't stick.

But real snow does. And that's what the world hungers for, something that sticks. Not something that's tossed by the wind."

The old man sat by the fire and stared at the crumbling logs. The flames flickered and glistened off the polished exterior of the golden pots and danced about the walls.

I tried to steer him from his tangent about the snow and focused on the utensils. "Those look old."

He nodded. "They are."

"What do you use them for? Popcorn?"

Again, his eyes twinkled. "Believe it or not, they're used to help the hopeless. Marriages with no future. Couples caught in the web of the past and present."

"You don't let couples bang each other in the head with them, do you?"

"Oh no, nothing like that!" We both laughed and Rue padded down the stairs and jumped onto the man's lap and snuggled.

"How can a couple of gold pots restore a marriage?"

"There are three, actually. I can show you how they can help, but there's something I need from you first."

"What's that?"

"You have to be willing."

"To do what?"

He leaned forward, his elbows on his knees, eyes piercing mine. "To hope. To change. These pots will open a new world. You can't be forced to look at them, but once you do, you can't help but respond."

"It sounds . . . strange."

He dipped his head. "I'm sure it does. And I wouldn't blame you if you didn't want to see. But if you choose to, there's something you have to do."

"Which is . . . "

"Be willing to *believe* in your marriage. That a future together is possible for you and your husband."

I shook my head. "I can't go there. Not after all we've been through."

He scratched the dog's back. "I understand. But one more question. I asked if there was another woman in your husband's life. But I haven't asked you if there is another man in yours."

My face flushed and I stirred up all the indignation I could muster. "I beg your pardon. Are you accusing me of something?"

He stared into my eyes.

"How can you accuse me of seeing another man when you don't even know me?"

He put the dog on the warm hearth and stood. "You're right. I'm meddling. Let me get the back bedroom ready for you."

"No, I can't stay." I threw off the cover and stood. "I have to get home to my children."

"Trust me. It's too dangerous to try and make it off the mountain tonight. The roads are next to impassable. As soon as the phone line is restored, you can call your family."

"What about your neighbors? Maybe their phones work."

"I checked with the nearest one while I was out. They don't have service either. I expect it might take a while to—"

In the middle of his sentence the lights flickered and went dark. Rue whimpered and jumped from the hearth.

There was still a faint, white light outside, but the entire house had gone dark. The man quickly went to the kitchen and returned with a flashlight and handed it to me. "Keep this with you. I have a few more just for such an occasion."

"This is spooky," I said.

"Oh, it happens often. Nothing to be worried about."

"No, I mean, it's weird. On our honeymoon the power went out. Not that we cared, but we were in the dark all night."

The man was silent. I could tell something was going on in his mind.

"I need to check on my wife," he said finally. "Then I'll get the fire started in your room. It should keep you warm if the electricity stays off."

The First Choice

The first-floor guestroom was past the kitchen at the back of the house, across the hall from the pantry. A brick fireplace covered one wall and more bookshelves lined the other. But the most arresting feature of the room was a four-poster bed complete with a canopy and curtains tied at the side. It looked like something out of some Victorian storybook. While the room was quaint and warm, I secretly wondered if this was where they placed the coffins.

The man saw me staring. "Everything in the house was donated. This bed came from a wealthy family. It was an heirloom from their grandparents."

"Nice donation."

"They felt indebted for the changes that came from their stay. They wanted to give back."

He placed some newspaper under the wood already in the fireplace and lit a match. There were other logs stacked on the hearth, and he told me to add as many as I needed through the night.

"The kitchen is open for you. Anything you need, make yourself at home. And there's a bell on the counter. Ring that and I'll come . . . well, not running, but as fast as I can go. I'll keep checking the weather through the night and keep an eye out for your husband."

I picked up the phone but heard nothing but an annoying buzz. Rue padded in and cocked his head at me.

"It appears someone would like to keep you company. There are some treats in the pantry across the hall. A couple of those will keep him busy. He loves to curl up at your feet."

"I'd like that," I said. I picked up the tiny dog and put him on the covers. He looked up at me and made a token gesture of licking. When the man left, Rue jumped down and followed.

"Wait, I don't even know your name," I said.

The man turned in the doorway. His voice crackled

like the fire. "My wife calls me Jay."

I went to the pantry and found a plastic tub of doggy treats and opened it. Rue came quickly, his feet clicking across the hardwood. I tossed the treat onto the bed and he whimpered until I picked him up and placed him there.

I walked back into the main room and watched Jay carrying a tray upstairs. When he reached the top he paused and looked down over the banister. He looked at me—no, almost through me.

"Do you need something else?"

Water filled my eyes and I felt something quiver inside. *What if I do give it a chance? What if I open up enough to consider there could be hope? Would that be enough?*

"Stay right there," he said. "I'll be right back down."

Jay removed the three pots from their resting place and arranged them in front of the fire. "Snow is God's way of cleaning the landscape. He makes everything new that way. But when it melts, it reveals what is underneath. What's hidden. What's true. Melting snow exposes. Each flake is like a choice we make, the choices piling on top of one another. Do you follow?"

"I suppose, in some metaphorical sense."

The firelight made his face look like a fiery sunset after a thunderstorm. "The choices you make lead your heart toward your husband or away; they are never inconsequential."

"Can't you just run parallel?"

"Have you ever tried to draw a straight line on your own? There's always a little bend there because none of us is perfect. So it may appear that you're moving parallel to each other when in fact you're moving apart or together."

"How does it work? The pots, I mean."

He took my empty mug from beside the chair and put the spent tea bag aside. "Gather some snow in this from outside. Scoop it with your hands into the cup. Tap it down, get as much as you can, even letting it spill over. Then bring it to me."

I slipped into my shoes that were now toasty and warm and headed outside. The wind howled and wet snow pelted the side of the house. Something moved in the darkness.

"Jacob?"

No response. I didn't have to go far to scoop the snow,

and as quickly as I did, the act felt like foolishness. This caretaker was probably certifiable. Maybe he had another unsuspecting traveler upstairs trapped in a closet. Or maybe it was Jacob. Why had I trusted this old man? Why had I let my heart be moved by his kind words, or think there could be any kind of hope?

I hurried inside, kicking my shoes back over the heating vent, even though it wasn't working. I comforted myself with the thought that serial killers don't have nice little dogs, they have vicious curs.

"Good," Jay said. "Now take the pan and put the snow inside and hold it over the fire."

I gave him a look I usually hold back from anyone but my husband and the child who drops a glass in my kitchen. "That's it? I'm supposed to melt snow and it'll change my life?"

He smiled like he had heard that before and handed me a wooden spoon. "Hold the pot over the fire and stir the melting snow. Just try."

"I don't have to click my heels and say there's no place like home?"

Crow's-feet at the corners of his eyes. Age spots on his hands. A knowing look. A nod.

I held the pot over the fire and the snow began that slow descent from white to clear, pooling on the edges, moving on its own like an iceberg in an angry ocean. I stirred and a faint echo of music floated upward, a concoction of songs from the past reaching my ears, like tufts of air from birds' wings. "Promises Made, Promises Broken," by Dan Fogelberg. I recognized others we heard during our dating years. Songs discovered, uncovered by a new generation. "Riddles of romance" that stirred my heart.

Steam rose like incense and swirled in the fireplace, hovering under the flue, and I felt myself slipping, swaying, and in one uncontrolled moment I was enveloped. I did not fall, jump, or transmigrate; the scene simply cloaked me, and I was wholly and irrevocably taken in by the experience.

Pictures from the past, images of children laughing, moments captured and frozen in time cascaded around me like snow, passing me — and suddenly came to life. Music and voices and color, like a vast collage of my life — a dog I had known as a child; puka shells worn in a ninth grade ensemble; buttered popcorn spilled at a theater; my best friend and me eating muffins late at night, smiling before the camera with muffin-stained teeth; me crying through *On Golden Pond*; a deafening concert in a sea of people near a stage . . .

"There he is," I said breathlessly. More of a gasp of recognition than a full sentence. There was my husband, a young man again, hair much darker and fuller—no receding hairline. Swarthy and lusty and full of life, and a smile that made my heart ache.

The years had chipped away at his smile, had taken the edges of what was once irrepressible. Many long years had passed since the sight of him had stirred anything deep within me.

As I watched, I realized there is within each of us an inner longing for a place and season of life we have known—when the future seemed to stretch ahead like some green pasture, inviting us, across the meadow and into the breadth and depth of life itself. The desire to find such a place resonates and reverberates, creating a passion for that which can never be relived. And yet, here I was, looking into the eyes of the man who captivated me in this season of delight.

"Marlee," he shouted across the quad. And before I could answer, a much younger version of me sprinted into his arms. I took myself in, the thin thighs, the width of the hips—or lack of width, and the strong embrace. The difference was striking—not the physical difference between my body then and now, though there did seem to be less sagging in strategic areas, but the way I moved toward him, let myself be held, allowed him entry to my very soul. There was no reserve. Freely I opened my arms and embraced. Similarly, he held nothing back, and the look on his face as he gathered me in was pure contentment.

"I missed you," he said, picking me up and turning in the sunlight.

"We had breakfast together this morning." I laughed.

"Exactly. It's been too long."

I will not be dishonest. Something in my stomach turned as I watched. I couldn't decipher whether this reaction was to the clinging love of two passion-struck college kids or the comparison of what has resulted from our attraction.

When I turned back to the scene, a misty vapor swathed me and I walked through it, searching for our former life. I found us walking near a familiar lake on a moonless summer night. Resting on that bench in the

middle of nowhere. We had pictures of this place on subsequent anniversaries with subsequent children in tow,
though we hadn't visited in the past five years. His words
came back, a waterfall of a memory. Fumbling with
a piece of paper to get it just right. My hands over my
mouth, trembling at his heartfelt proposal.

I wanted to scream, to yell "caution"—to stop the
events about to unfold. The giving of the ring, down
on one knee, tears of happiness, and another long embrace that melted into a kiss so passionate I turned away.
When I looked again, we had moved from lake shadows
to candlelight in the little church where we were married.
The gown, the smooth skin, the trim figures underneath
the dress and tux, and the voice of our pastor charging us
to love until "death do us part."

Jacob had written his own vows. His deep, resonant
voice cut through time and with emotion he said, "Your
love has captured my heart. As long as it beats in my
chest, I pledge to let nothing come between the love we
will share in the years ahead. For it will take death's cold
embrace to separate us."

My eyes shut tight. We *had* loved until death. Unfor-
tunately it was love that died.

When I opened my eyes it was our first anniversary. Friends had given us a weekend stay at their mountain hideaway. A remote, snow-covered area where we had to park and hike the nearly mile-long driveway. There was nothing to keep us occupied but the stocked refrigerator, a few VHS movies, and each other. For some reason, having nothing to do didn't bother me.

We were still in love back then, content in finding pleasure in each other's bodies, and in our exuberance I knocked something from the shelf above the bed. As if peering over some forbidden parapet, the two of us pulled ourselves to the headboard and, mouths agape, looked in horror at the antique snow globe in a puddle on the wooden floor.

"How are we ever going to explain that?" I said.

Jacob laughed. I giggled, thinking about how the conversation might go. Then we were in each other's arms again, delighting and wading deeper into the waters of pleasure God had created for us.

The next scene was the result of one of those marital forays into the unknown—the arrival of our oldest, Becca. My heart, not in part but the whole, leapt and beat furiously. I said some awful things to my husband during that delivery. He just smiled and held my hand as I struggled through those hours. I always thought I didn't really mean those things. He forgave me without question.

As I watched, the rush of memory aroused an unwelcome internal conflict. I didn't want to be drawn to him, but I was, particularly when I saw his wonderment at tiny fingers and toes, heard the suckling sounds of my firstborn daughter at my breast, and drank in the wonder of a newborn.

"She's so . . . perfect," Jacob said. He reached out a finger and she grasped it as she suckled.

"She's amazing," I whispered.

Two people united around a shared infant. We were together. He even changed diapers, much to my surprise. And never complained about my nesting and the shuffling of furniture, and the crib I returned three times and exchanged because it just wasn't right for the room.

"Children are a gift from God Himself," Jay said. He was near me, watching the same scenes. My cheeks flushed as I turned to face him, and Justin ran past me, chased by a much older Becca. My husband, a little older and more harried than in his college days, trailed the kids, carrying David.

"Can you see this?" I said to Jay, looking into the mist around me. Wondering how much of the anniversary scene he had witnessed.

"Don't focus on me. Stay in the moment. Drink it all in because it won't be here long."

When I turned back to my family, my husband and I were sitting together on the couch, Christmas wrapping paper strewn about the house, Becca playing "panthers and cheetahs" with the boys, their little legs scurrying downstairs, yipping and yapping in an incomprehensible children's game. A smile passed between us as we listened to their imaginations fly.

"Where do you think we'll be in ten years?" Jacob said.

"Under a tree surrounded by wrapping paper."

He laughed. "No, where do you want to be?"

"Someplace warm where we can listen to this," I said, the noise of the panthers and cheetahs rising toward us.

"I want to give you that and more," he said, leaning over and giving a kiss. "I'll clean up down here and watch them. Why don't you make use of these. You deserve it."

He handed me the unwrapped bath oils he had helped the kids pick out. Lavender and rose, my favorite get-away fragrances.

"No, I need to get lunch started," I said.

He shook his head. "Upstairs. Now. The wildebeests will survive."

"Panthers and cheetahs," I corrected.

"Go."

Had he really been that thoughtful?

The warmth and noise quickly faded, and in a blink Becca was nearly grown. We were in the car heading to soccer practice.

"Why do you and Dad fight so much?" she said.

I stared out the windshield. "We don't really fight; we just disagree about a lot of things."

"You fight," she said. "And you don't make up. It's like a teakettle that's always ready to boil anytime the heat's turned up."

I gripped the steering wheel a little tighter. "That must feel bad to live with every day."

"Yeah."

It felt like the scene in *Citizen Kane* where the husband and wife are sitting at opposite ends of the dining room table, the years flitting by, and the distance grow-ing between them. The more I poured into our home and family life, the more Jacob seemed to pour into his work. The resentment festered. There we were, snow falling outside, him staring at the Sports page, me star-ing at the Obituaries.

"Dan Fogelberg died," I said.

Jacob didn't even drop the paper and look at me. "What from? Accident?"

"Prostate cancer."

"Shame. He wasn't that old, was he?"

"Fifty-six."

"Remember 'Leader of the Band'?"

I nodded, but he didn't see me. He hid behind his paper—except I noticed he wasn't reading the sports any longer. He was just staring off, out the window, hid-den behind the football standings. I moved toward him through the mist, shocked that there was more going on in his head than scores and statistics.

"We saw him once, didn't we?" he said. "In Cincinnati?"

I answered vacantly, telling him the name of the town and venue. He could have told me how much the tickets were, of course. But he kept staring, finally lowering the paper and looking my way. I was already gone. I had shut him out. Decided conversation wasn't worth the time.

He pulled the paper up and I heard a voice amplified through speakers. We were sitting in a large church with a few hundred couples, listening to a man talk about going deeper in our marriage. I sat beside him in rapt attention taking notes. He glanced my way, nervously twirling his wedding band. I gave a look at his empty conference notebook, then back to my own. I thought he was uninterested in our marriage, at making it work. But when I looked more closely, there was something written in the book. I strained to see it at the bottom of the page, but he closed it quickly.

And then we were saying good-bye to the children earlier that afternoon. David held on tightly to me, and I choked back the tears as I heard myself tell how soon we would be home. The door closed and the three children went to the window to watch us.

"Where are they going?" David said.

"Probably more Christmas shopping," Justin said.

"Yeah, probably more shopping," Becca said, putting a hand on their shoulders. Her face was the last thing I saw as the mist engulfed the scene.

Drifting, floating, swirling like vapor rising, the mist parted and I saw the empty pot over the fire. Jay pulled my hand back and rested the pot on the brick fireplace. I was too stunned to speak. To see your own life vaporize before you that way, to see your own children struggling with the choices made, even though they didn't understand them, took my breath away.

"It felt real. Like I was right there. Every bit of it."

"You have beautiful children," Jay said.

"You saw it too. How?"

"I can only observe, but the one holding the handle controls the experience. Those were your memories. It was your life."

"But I didn't experience some of it. I didn't know what my children said. I didn't know my husband had written anything down in that notebook."

He nodded. "The answers to the questions you now have will surface from the snow."

"What do you mean?"

"The hope you have for your marriage will lead you forward. The snow will show you the truth. Your mind will guide you from one memory to the next. The questions you have now, the observations you made, and frankly, your openness, all combine to lead you to what you're really seeking."

"But I told you, we've made up our minds. It's over."

"Yes, but you also said you would give my hope for you a chance. The images spring from a desire for change."

I looked at the warm pot on the hearth and the two that awaited me. "I want to check the phone. Try to call the children."

"That's fine," Jay said.

"I don't think I can go any further," I said as I reached the hall. "It's too painful . . . too much emotion."

"I know. But part of you wants to know more. Part of you wants to hope."

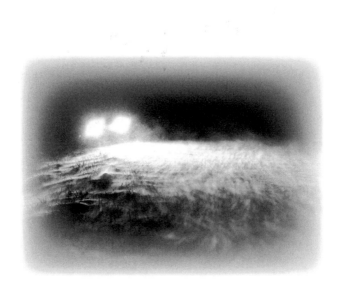

The *Other* Man

The phone was stillborn. As lifeless as my soul. I put the handset on the cradle and thought of Jacob's face as he fought the wheel coming around the curve, saw the oncoming headlights, and I closed my eyes again, awaiting impact. He was still out there somewhere. He wouldn't have left me alone to freeze. Or would he?

A bay window near the kitchen table looked out on the landscape. I imagined fragile couples sitting here over fresh cups of coffee and warm biscuits, repairing their marriages a meal at a time. I shone my flashlight through the window and gasped at the piling snow. Wet, thick flakes as big as my hand fell fast and straight. Tree limbs swayed and quivered under the weight.

On the kitchen table sat a plastic Tupperware tub, the kind the kids used for popcorn at one of their "sleep-overs." Jacob would pop the corn, Becca would melt butter, and Justin and David were ready with enough sea salt to raise blood pressures in two states. Laughing, giggling, they would hurry off to the family room to watch one of the latest from Pixar or an old horror movie Jacob loved to show them. Frankenstein or Dracula or the Wolfman.

I took the bowl and opened the side door. Without thinking, I stepped onto the porch in my socks. There was a sitting area here, too, with several tables and chairs. I scooped the snow into the bowl from the tabletop and kept going until it was overflowing.

Glancing up, I saw a light on in the window above me and the flutter of a curtain. Then, nothing but the stillness of the night and the falling snow.

Jay was at the back door when I returned. "You forgot something," he chuckled, looking at my feet. No scolding or chiding, just a friendly recognition of the truth. He took the bowl from me and sat it on the table. I handed him my wet socks, and he met me in the living room with a towel and another pair. The feeling returned to my feet and I was warm again and ready for another excursion.

I took the second pot from the hearth and dumped the snow inside, making sure to drain every drop into the pan. I did not want to miss anything. I did not want to come out of the misty scenes too quickly.

"If the first bowl plumbed my past and used my own experiences and mind, how can it know the truth of the present?"

Jay's face reflected the firelight, orange and intense. "The snow will only show you what is. It covers the truth and then reveals it."

"So you don't know how it works either."

His eyes sparkled. "Just that it has never failed in all our years."

I took the pot and held it near the fire. "Your wife. What's wrong with her? Why does she stay upstairs?"

"Believe me, if she could come down, she would be right at your side. It's just her stage of life."

I wanted to ask more questions, how long they'd been married, how long he had cared for her, how many people had gone through what I was doing, but the curiosity of the golden bowl beckoned and I thrust it onto the fire. I closed my eyes as the mist ascended and the power of the snow enveloped me.

Music had taken me to the threshold of my past, but this time I heard a voice crackling through a tinny speaker. It gave an ominous weather forecast, a freak storm that had taken the region by surprise. Equally ominous traffic reports told of motorists stranded in cars and urged everyone to stay inside and not venture out.

"Shhh!" Becca said. She was huddled in the living room with her brothers under a cover they had dragged from my bed.

"Why don't we just watch a movie," David said.

"There's no electricity, dope," Justin said. "That's why we can't turn on the lights."

"Then how can we hear the radio?"

"It uses batteries, goofball."

"Quiet!" Becca said. She pulled the radio closer and turned up the volume.

The newscaster gave a list of closed roads and many accidents. Her cell phone rang and she fumbled in her pocket and opened it. "Mom?"

"No, it's your aunt Susan. Becca, have you heard anything from your mom and dad?"

"Not yet. And the electricity went off."

"I figured. We've been trying the home line for a while."

Becca got up from the couch and walked out of earshot of the boys who kicked at each other from opposite sides of the couch.

"Aunt Susan," Becca said softly. "I'm scared."

"Your dad's a good driver. They're probably stuck somewhere in a bad cell area and—"

"No, I don't mean that. I'm worried about them, but I'm scared something's happening. There was a letter on Dad's desk. From a lawyer. I opened it."

"Oh Becca. I'm so sorry. I'm sure they'll work it out."

"No, it's talking about a divorce and papers and their agreement. I don't understand most of it but it looks like it's a done deal. Do you know anything about this?"

Silence on the other end. "Honey, I wish I could drive down there right now and be with you. I'm so sorry. We've been praying for your mom and dad, and I knew things were bad. I didn't know they'd hired a lawyer."

Tears streamed down Becca's face. "Why are they doing this?"

A pause on the other end. "Honey, you have to pull together for your brothers. Let's just get you through tonight and we'll deal with all of this. Together. Do you understand?"

Hearing my sister talk this way to my daughter gave me a chill. We had never been what I would call "close," but I could tell Becca was comforted by her words. Susan was acting in my stead, providing the support and comfort I couldn't.

The boys were ratcheting up the noise, then David came running in with his blanket wrapped around him and bumped into the doorjamb and fell. Wails pierced the room.

"Justin!" Becca yelled.

"I didn't do anything!"

"I have to go, Aunt Susan."

"Call me if you hear anything."

"I will."

"And know that we're praying for you."

"Thank you." Becca hung up and gathered David in her arms and dragged him to the living room. "We have to work together to get through this. Mom and Dad are stuck somewhere."

"Are they going to be okay?" David asked, sniffling.

Hearing his concern broke my heart.

"They'll be fine, but they can't call right now. So we have to stick together. I want you to go upstairs and get all your covers. We'll push the couch and love seat together and make a big tent in the living room to keep us warm."

"Yes!" Justin said.

"But what about Santa?" David said. "If we're in the living room, he won't come, will he?"

Justin snickered and Becca ignored him. She sounded just like me when she said, "He won't care, if we're asleep."

"But how will he see the tree if the lights don't work?"

Justin rolled his eyes. "The guy can come to every house on the planet and squeeze through a chimney, and you're worried he won't be able to see?"

She flicked on a flashlight and gave it to David. "Just get your covers and hurry back. No fighting. And watch your step coming down."

The two were off in a flash and Becca hit her contact list on her cell. She chose both my phone and Jacob's and texted, "We're ok. Wherever u r, be safe."

She hit the send button and closed the phone. She looked out the front window at the falling snow and more tears came. She wiped them away quickly as the boys clambered downstairs.

I turned away from the scene, overwhelmed by her emotion and resolve. I wanted to reach out, to write a message on the window or call out, but I couldn't break through. When I looked again, Becca was gone and there were my parents, dressed in their Sunday best, sitting close to each other in a Christmas Eve service at their retirement home. There were perhaps twenty people attending, all dressed in bright reds and greens. When the pastor, who was wearing khakis and a polo shirt, asked if there were any prayer requests, several hands went up. My mother clutched a wad of tissues in one hand and lifted it when the man asked if there were any unspoken requests. He nodded as if he understood. She raised the tissues to her face, and my father put an arm around her and pulled her close.

It did not dawn on me until that moment, but if I was seeing what was happening in real time, I might also be able to find Jacob. I looked back at the golden pot and shook it, some of the water slapping out and hissing on the burning wood.

"Careful," Jay said beside me, but I struggled to stay focused on the misty steam until a building came into view. Through the snow and foggy window I saw a man pacing, looking out from his book-lined office. On the desk were white pages in various piles, with sticky "sign here" notes. He glanced at his watch, then pulled out his cell phone and dialed a number.

"This is not what I want to see," I said to Jay. "I want to know where my husband is."

"Don't try to control it," he said. "You'll learn by simply observing."

The next scene was my sister's home. She and her husband in their bedroom closet, wrapping paper and presents around them, were deep in prayer. For us. For our marriage. It was humbling and humiliating.

"You have people who care for you," Jay said.

Engulfed in the mist again, the water bubbling and frothing, another home with few books and more linoleum came into view. A figure sat at a makeshift computer table, a TV blaring a football game in the background. A beer in one hand and a mouse in the other, he navigated through his Facebook contacts. I closed my eyes.

"Do you know him?" Jay said.

"He's a friend I knew in high school."

"But you've become reacquainted."

"Only online. It's nothing, really. Found his picture on Facebook and friended him."

The longer we lingered at Erik's house, with Erik typing a message with two fingers, the more interested Jay became and the more uncomfortable I grew. I let the pot slip from the fire, but Jay held my hand there.

"Wishing you a warm and happy Christmas Eve," Erik wrote. "Hoping things go well with the kids in the coming days. Hoping there are better times ahead for you. Love, Erik."

"He didn't get a good grade in typing class," I joked.

Jay remained focused. "He doesn't write like he's just an old friend."

"We've had some conversations over the past few months," I said, and there was something hollow to my voice.

"Did you date in high school?"

"A little. We were just kids."

"But you've made a connection now."

"I have lots of Facebook friends."

"How many of them sent you greetings on Christmas Eve? On your anniversary? On the day you were going to sign divorce papers?"

I didn't answer. Instead, I watched Erik crumple his beer can and toss it in the trash, then reach for another in the minifridge under the makeshift table.

"Have you met face-to-face?"

"Just at our reunion. It was innocent. He's just being nice to think of me and write."

"Something happened in your eyes when you saw him. When you read his message, a light went on."

I nodded. "All right, I'll admit there's a spark. Just remembering those early years. The youthful infatuation. Mental gymnastics about the past. Wondering how things might have wound up if . . . "

"If you had chosen that life instead of this one," Jay said. "And whether or not it's too late to still choose?"

"I guess the thought crossed my mind that we could have a life together. He's coming off a bad relationship. He learned a lot from it," I added, realizing I sounded defensive.

"Like controlling his drinking."

"Yeah, well, I didn't know about that. He must have stock in Coors." The scene lingered and I tried to talk to mask my discomfort. Laughing at some unharnessed memory of Erik when we were young.

"Marlee, you have a good chance at happiness. You have great kids. Your family loves you. Cares for you. The best hope for lifelong love is not with anyone but the one you said 'I do' to."

"My best chance died years ago, then. Jacob looks at us as another investment gone bad. He would probably stay together to save the legal hassle and to keep the kids under one roof, but he won't even fight anymore. He's at the *whatever* stage. Whatever happens now is fine with him. He's emotionally checked out. He's engrossed in his work. He's not there anymore. And frankly, I'm glad."

Jay didn't speak and thankfully the scene changed again, this time to a dark, snowy field. I couldn't make out much of the scenery because it was snow covered.

"Is that around here?" I said.

"I can't tell," Jay said. "Wait a minute. That looks like someone's shoe sticking out of the snow."

My breath caught and I choked out the words. "It's

his. It's Jacob's."

I scanned the scene and through the flurries noticed some trees, an incline, and a fence post. "I know this place. It's right below where our car spun out."

Jay jumped up and rushed to the front hallway, throwing his coat on. I followed, but he told me to stay with the fire. Stay with the scene.

With tears in my eyes I said, "I thought I tripped over a rock. It must have been him. He was trying to come here."

"I'll find him," Jay said. "You stay here."

"No, I have to go with you."

"Marlee . . . " He put a hand on my shoulder and I felt something warm coursing through my body. A connection with the past and present? "Stay here. I'll be right back."

Shaking, still holding the pot, I placed it back over the fire as Jay left. The water grew warm again and steam washed over me. I closed my eyes, wondering if Jacob could still be alive. He needed medical help, but with the phone out and no cell I couldn't imagine what we could do.

The scene was the pasture again and Jacob's shoe

moved under the covering of snow. A good sign. *"Get up,"* I whispered.

Headlights shone on the road above, and then a terrible sound of rubber on ice, trying to grip, trying to stop the momentum of the downhill slide. The car careered into the thin trees above, headlights wobbling over the snow, then toppled over the hillside toward my husband.

The steam sizzled and evaporated in front of me. I put the pot down and ran to the back door, looking over the landscape. I could see nothing through the storm, not even headlights.

Frantic, I scooped snow from the back patio into the plastic bowl and ran back to the fire, pouring it quickly into the bowl and jamming it on top of the fire and holding it close until the white began to melt.

"Come on," I whispered.

Something moved behind me. Rue was back, sniffing and whining at the garage door. When I turned back to the fire, the steam rose and I entered without any thought to the process, whether this would work or not. I peered into the wafting vapor, looking for my husband and the old man who would be his paramedic and savior.

But I did not see the pasture.

The Mistake

A woman with long, brown hair carried a feverish child back and forth across the kitchen in a small apartment. The baby's croupy cough startled me, the chest rattling like marbles in a tin box. A vaporizer sat by an empty crib and the woman pulled the child close. By the window was a scraggly Christmas tree draped with a secondhand garland.

When she turned, I recognized something in the face. Was this me years earlier with Becca? I didn't recognize the apartment. Had I chosen the wrong gold pot?

A phone rang and as the woman picked it up, the baby began a crying, coughing, wail. "His fever is up. I can't get it down. I don't know what to do."

The voice. *Her* voice. My own daughter was a mother.

"No, I'm not calling her," Becca said. A pause at something said on the other end. "I don't care if she could help, I'm not calling her."

Slowly, the scene in the apartment faded and I was in a loud, dark room filled with laughter and music and people shaking off snow on the wet, wooden floor. At a table in the corner, raising two drinks toward each other and clinking glasses, were two young men, ruddy and handsome, grizzled with a week's growth of beard.

"To another Christmas Eve," the younger one said. "It's good to see you."

"Same here," the other said, taking a long pull on the drink.

Silence between them. Not much eye contact.

"Feels like yesterday, doesn't it?"

"What? The accident?"

The man nodded. "Twenty years ago tonight. Our lives changed forever."

A glance at the table. "Yeah. Wonder how Becca is tonight."

"I don't think she and her husband are doing well, to be honest."

"Can't say I'm surprised, can you?"

The younger one shook his head. "You okay?"

Another long pull and a shrug. "Sure, as long as I have one of these in my hand." He stared at the glass. "If I had to be honest, I'd say I feel lost. Like there are a thousand roads to choose and every one of them leads to a dead end. Every time I hear snow forecast or see the lights flicker during a power outage, I'm right back there in the living room under those covers."

"Christmas was never the same after that year, was it."

A nod. He drained the glass.

"Have you talked with Mom lately?" David asked.

"No. Still hard to get past everything that happened."

"Yeah. But it's been twenty years. Maybe it's time."

"Can I get you two something else?" a pretty waitress said, bouncing in place as she stood by the table.

"Time for a couple more of these," Justin said.

"Be right back," she said.

The maelstrom at the bar and the two at the booth faded, along with the peanut shells and booming music. Though I wanted to see my husband, I had stumbled onto something entirely different and unexpected.

As if seeing my children wasn't enough, the next scene

took my breath away. Jacob, the husband of my youth, was much older and stoop-shouldered. His face was stubble-filled and ravaged by time. His skin was spotted and wrinkled and there was a darkness to his eyes, something vacant. He ate his meal in silence and sat by a small tabletop Christmas tree. Scattered pictures lay on the coffee table. Images of what had been.

I noticed nothing significant about the scene until he stood. Moving from the table to the kitchen was a Herculean effort. His right leg was almost useless as he dragged it beside him. He was missing fingers on both hands. I reached out in the shadows but made no connection.

"Oh Jacob," I said.

And then I was gone, through the swirling snow again, inserted into another scene of a woman putting away groceries. Even though I did not see the face, I knew her. You can always tell your own figure in a view from behind. If I had compared the slender hips of my youth to the ones of midlife, I was now comparing them to twenty years in the future. Gravity had continued its work, but I felt a certain pride at my appearance. My hair was shorter, grayer in places, mainly at the roots, my arms a little flabby underneath, and when I turned

I noticed the lines in my face and extra skin at my neck that could have used tightening. All in all, not bad if going strictly on a score of physical attributes. What concerned me most was the look on my face.

A sound of announcers and cheering came from the living room. The unmistakable cacophony of televised football. At the bottom of the grocery pile was a case of beer, and no sooner had I put away the other bags than a much more portly Erik waddled into the kitchen.

"Hope you didn't run the heater in the back." He ripped open the box and felt the cans, then cursed. "These go in the fridge downstairs. And could you bring up the rest of the Coors when you come back?"

It was at least a request and not an order, but something about the way I acquiesced to his demand made my jaw drop. Then, as he walked out, I muttered something as I picked up the case of beer.

"What was that?" he said, turning.

"Nothing."

"No, what did you say?" Erik stood in the doorway, where he could both yell at me and have a good view of the unfolding game. I couldn't believe what I was seeing. The kind and considerate man who had sent e-mails and supportive messages was now staring me down.

As I bent to pick up the case, he grabbed my arm. "Don't ignore me. Tell me what you said."

"Nothing," I begged, tears in my eyes, trembling. There was real fear here, as if this were only the latest salvo. Perhaps this contributed to the hollow in my eyes. "Please, let me go. I'll be right back."

"You'd better be," he spat.

Glancing around the kitchen, I noticed pictures of the three children in inconspicuous places, hiding here and there, as if there was a moratorium on the past leaking into the present. Something in my stomach twinged, like a light of knowledge being flicked on, and I saw what no one could tell me about the greener grass on the other side of the relational fence. Like taking some wild animal into our home and trying to domesticate it. The only life in the home was not the sound of children or grandchildren, but a football battle and the occasional belch. And me trudging back up the steps with the remaining case of beer for the man of my dreams. How had this happened? Had I spent twenty years with . . . him?

❧

The steam sizzled and fizzled and Rue stood by my side, watching the last of the snow vaporize into the air. I placed the pot by the hearth and took a breath. Anxious thoughts swirled like the raging storm. I ran to the back window looking for any sign of life or light. I found neither, just darkness. I checked the phone again. Dead. I found my flashlight and checked the garage. Jay's car was gone and the door was still up. Snow had piled and drifted over three feet deep with a set of tracks down the middle of the driveway. In the other bay sat a Suburban, and I assumed it was four-wheel drive.

Helpless, I watched Rue run up the steps and disappear around the corner at the top. I followed, my footsteps echoing throughout the house. The wooden floor was slick and cold as I crept along. Using my flashlight I checked the hall and found on either side of it were rooms with six-panel, closed doors. Instead of numbers there were words on each. "Goodness," "Peace," "Patience," and several others words I recognized in the list of fruits of the Spirit. (I don't know a lot about the Bible, but I remembered those.) I opened one that said "Joy" and peered at a bright, cheery room with a yellow comforter on the king-sized bed and wallpaper patterned with sunshine and rainbows. Just looking at it made me smile. A handcrafted needlepoint depicted a basket of fruit and underneath said, "But the fruit of the Spirit is . . . joy." A healthy number of books about marriage lined the shelves, as well as a few novels.

I closed the door and moved to the end of the hall where another door stood open a few inches, just wide enough for Rue to slip through. On the outside was the word "Peace." A thin sliver of light hit the hallway floor and I paused to listen. A whispered voice inside floated about the hallway like a snowflake too light to fall. It sounded like a prayer from a person straining with each breath. "Give me the strength to face this trial," the woman said. Then more I couldn't hear.

After a moment of silence I called out, "Hello?" Rue trotted to the door and looked out, his ears straight and pointed. "I'm sorry to bother you."

"Come in," she said. Her voice was like gravel.

I pushed the door open and Rue stepped back, then hurried to a chair in the corner and jumped onto the bed. There was a fire in the hearth and the room lit with a golden glow. I turned off the flashlight and held it at my side. Another comfortable chair sat by the fire and a nightstand held a worn Bible. More books lined the shelves along a wall. I recognized the dresser immediately, for it was the same kind my mother had handed down to me. The wallpaper was sky blue, and the firelight made the room feel warm and cozy.

"You must be Marlee," the woman said, her white hair barely above the comforter line. She was snuggled into a mountain of covers.

"And you're Jay's wife?" I said, moving closer.

"I've been expecting you," she said. "He told me what happened. Pull the chair over here so I can see you as we talk."

"I can't stay. I just wanted to ask if I could take your other car to look for my husband. Jay left to find him and I'm concerned."

With much effort, she pulled herself up to a sitting position. It was darker on this side of the room, but I could make out her features in the flickering light. Her hair was white and her face wrinkled, like the crumpled paper of a perfectionistic writer. Her hands were knuckles and veins, and the skin hung on her like an old coat. Her face was pallid and she licked her lips with a tongue that seemed swollen and searching for moisture.

"Would you mind handing me that glass of water?" she said, her finger shaking as she pointed to the night-stand inches away.

I held it for her and she drank a few sips from a straw like a child, smacking her lips and nodding. She took a deep breath before she said, "Thank you."

I returned the glass to the stand and she asked if the storm had slowed. When I turned back, there was something about her face and the concern there that seemed familiar. A spark in the eyes that moved me with a flicker of recognition.

"I don't think it's slowing at all. And I'm worried about my husband. Yours, too."

"You can use the car. He usually keeps the keys on a pegboard in the garage." Her words came slowly, with effort, as if she wanted to say something more but held back for some reason.

When I turned to go she stuck out an arthritic hand and took my wrist. Something electric shot through me, a sensory experience I had never felt, as if some forbidden conduit of mercy had taken hold.

"What is it?" the woman said. "Something's troubling you. Something you've seen."

Searching her eyes was like looking into a rising ocean. Her eyebrows raised before I could speak, then came a knowing smile.

"So, my husband has shown you the power of snow."

"Yes, and I've seen something awful."

"You saw the future?"

"The third pan. I put the snow in it by mistake . . ." My voice trailed and the room felt as if it were spinning. "The last scene of the present showed an accident and in my hurry, I got the wrong pot."

"It's all right. I'm just sorry you had to go through that alone."

"I n-need to know," I stammered. "Is what I saw what *might be* or what *will be*? I want to know if it has to be this way, or if the future can be changed."

"And you want to know if it can change, how do *you* change it?"

"Yes. Exactly."

She blinked, like a female Yoda, then closed her eyes and lifted a finger in the air and traced something unseen. "Just one snowflake changes the construction of the water. One choice changes the construction of a life. What feels like an accident changes everything. Like that snow globe you broke on your anniversary."

"How did you know about that?" I said. I hadn't told even my closest friends the story. And we bought a replica of the globe and never told the owners the truth.

She kept her eyes closed and her hand fell to rest on the comforter. The woman moved her legs under the covers and Rue stretched and curled his tongue, his legs shaking as he extended every inch. Then he snuggled close again.

When I looked back at the woman's face, she was smiling, showing aged teeth, and it was in that smile that I finally recognized. The chipped tooth. The faded brown eyes. Her face was a mirror that projected forward in time.

I saw myself.

I stepped back, trying to breathe, questions swirling. "This can't be . . . you can't be . . . "

"I am."

"But, if you are . . . then Jay . . . is Jacob?"

"He is."

"But why didn't I recognize him? How could I have been so blind?"

"Remember the story of the two on the road to

Emmaus?" she said.

That sounded biblical. Something about a post-resurrection appearance and travelers, but I couldn't place it.

"They didn't recognize the one they loved as they walked along," she said. "Their eyes were closed because of their own pain. And then they sat down by a fire and He kept speaking to them. He opened their eyes with His words and their hearts burned within them.

"Tell me," she continued. "Did the things you saw in the melting snow make your heart yearn for another chance? For a different outcome to your life?"

"Yes," I choked.

She looked inside my soul and held out both hands. "Then this is it. What you see here is just as possible as what you saw in the snow. Neither is reality yet. But you can choose."

I sat on the bed, the air escaping the room. "But there's so much hurt. So much distance between him and me. It's not like we can just start over."

"You think I don't know that? I know what you've been through."

I stared at the fire, wondering why it didn't flicker and die. You have to have wood to keep a fire going. You have to have hope to keep a marriage intact.

"So, you're not real? You're just like the woman I saw who married Erik?"

Though her body had been ravaged by time, that could not steal the sudden sweetness to her face or her words. "You have been given a gift few are open to receiving. You have seen two different futures, two differing paths for what may lie ahead."

"*May*," I said. "So it's not determined. The future can be changed."

"Yes. But what might be, never will be, unless you make the choice to move toward your husband. What could be, will never be known if it's abandoned. You'll never experience the joy and tenderness of a lifelong love unless you fight for it. I know that now. The question is, will you? Or will you settle for something else?"

"The children," I said. "What will their lives be like in your version of the future?"

"Children struggle no matter what you choose," she said. "*Their* choices matter as well. But I can assure you they will be affected by what you decide tonight."

Something warm but terrifying spread through me, like hot chocolate . . . or more like radiation. And fear rose up with the fallout of my thoughts.

"I've been trying so hard. I've been working at the relationship for so long."

"It's not about trying harder. In the end, it's not really about you doing the right thing or him responding in the right way. It's letting go of your own limited vision. This is not about what you can dredge up from the floor of your imagination. It's allowing God to do something you can't. That's what it's always been about. For the two on the road two thousand years ago, and the men on the road tonight."

"So I have a chance to get this right . . . "

She shook her head. "Not get it right. It's about making good choices. It's putting one foot in front of the other on a good path, one that will lead you to a place down the road you can be proud of, no matter what response you get."

"I'm confused. You're not promising a husband who buys a dog and serves me soup? A man who wants to help other struggling marriages? You can't be sure that will happen?"

"There are two futures and infinite possibilities ahead. You can move toward one or the other right now, with every choice you make. But you will never know what might become of your marriage, what life you might give to others, if you don't take a step."

Rue sat up on the bed, his ears pricked again, looking out the window. Through the blinding snow I saw a hint of yellow flashers lighting the darkness.

"Who chose his name?" I said, nodding toward the dog.

"Jacob," she said. "One of the regrets he had. Just shows that a regret can become a good thing when a good choice is made."

I gave the dog a pat on the head and placed a hand on the woman's arm. "I don't understand all of this. But thank you."

She smiled. "Now hurry along. Get to them. You've already made your choice. I can tell."

I looked back once at the doorway, the dog spread out on the covers and her hand on top of its head. A picture that stayed with me as I ran down the stairs in the dark, the fire in the living room hearth nearly out. My shoes were dry, and I hurried and wrapped myself in my thin coat. I found the keys and managed to get the garage door up, hitting the manual release. The huge vehicle moved through the deep snow like a turtle, then gained speed and went off the edge of the concrete driveway as I slipped and slid down toward the road. With the Suburban in four-wheel drive, I spun the wheels, trying to give myself enough momentum to move, but not so much that I would lose control.

The road was deserted, the previous tire tracks almost completely covered by the blowing snow. In my rearview mirror I noticed the soft glow of light coming from the second-floor window, and then the house disappeared through the trees and the curtain of snow. It took several minutes to find the main road, then I took the right turn too quickly and my back end fishtailed. I spun into the turn and slid, then regained control and moved back to the middle of the road and down the hill.

Her words, *my words*, echoed as I drove. *One choice changes the construction of a life. You'll never experience the joy and tenderness of a lifelong love unless you fight for it.*

Snowflakes, like choices, splashed on the windshield. I hit the high beams and the view was no better. It was actually worse, the flakes descending in waves now, the wind whipping them sideways across the covered road. I have never heard of a snow tsunami, but if there was such a thing I was in the middle of it.

I hit the brake down a steep slope and went into a slide to the right, pine trees by the edge of the road coming dangerously close. I let off the brake, thinking I was headed over the embankment, but the car held and righted itself. I was concentrating so hard on keeping my momentum without plunging over the edge that I didn't see the yellow flashers until I was on top of them. Only two choices — I could swerve or hit the brake and hope. Instinctively I hit the brake pedal.

The road dipped to the right and as soon as I put my foot down, the car slid toward the curve, toward the flashing yellow. Windshield wipers going full tilt, my front end pulled to the right and my headlights shone on the overturned car in the field, more flashing yellow.

In a split second, through the deluge of snow, I saw faces of my children, my mother and father, my sister and brother-in-law praying, and my husband. Jacob peered through the driver's side window of the car. Beside him was Jay, the older, wiser, more compassionate version of him. They shrank back and braced for impact, and their two faces became one.

"No!" I shouted, unable to steer or stop the car. I threw

up my hands, covered my eyes, and for the first time in as long as I could remember released a prayer from the heart. "God help me! Show me what to do."

Chorus

That prayer was the last thing I remembered before opening my eyes. The surroundings blurry, I recognized a voice before I saw any face.

"Mom!" Becca shouted. "She's awake! She's back!"

Becca wasn't older with a crying baby, she was my daughter again. David and Justin were beside her, held back from the hospital bed, wide-eyed and struggling to get to me. They hugged me as best they could, through the wires and monitors. My head felt like it had been twisted around and smacked with a tire iron a few times. I lifted a hand to my face and felt a bandage that wrapped around my forehead. My mouth was parched and I reached an IV-laden hand to the nightstand to get a drink. Instead,

Becca got the glass and held the straw to my lips. The flash of memory was all I needed for my eyes to go blurry again, this time with tears.

"We were worried, Mom," David said. "The lights went out and when you didn't come home we were all alone."

"Becca did a good job of taking care of us, though," Justin said.

Becca's eyes twinkled as she stood watching, pulling her hair behind one ear and feigning disinterest at what the boys said. It was like looking in a mirror at myself.

"You guys did great," I said. "Bringing those covers downstairs and pulling the couches together."

"How did you know that?" Justin said.

I paused. "Well, I just figured you did that."

A nurse came in and the children moved back to let her check my vital signs. She wore a name tag that said, "Amanda."

"How do you feel, Mrs. Ebenezer?" She strapped something onto my arm, listened with her stethoscope and looked me in the eyes.

"Really good, considering," I said. "Really good. How long have I been out? What day is this?"

"It's Christmas Day," David said. "You need to come

home so we can open presents."

"We're going to check out your mom and make sure she's okay first, big guy," Amanda said. "Pulse is good. Blood pressure is good."

"They say you have a percussion," David said.

"Concussion," Justin corrected.

"Is that so?" I said. "Well, my head feels more like a drum that's been whacked, so percussion sounds right to me."

"How's the pain?" Amanda kept looking at my eyes. "On a scale of 1 to 10."

"I'm about a 5." I sat up slowly and my head spun. "And I think I want to go home."

Amanda smiled. "We're going to take care of your percussion first. Just lay back."

I took her advice and put my head firmly on the pillow, turning to the window and watching a lazy snowfall outside. The blizzard was over and the remnant flakes fell like stragglers to the dance. Suddenly, a wave of panic swept over me and I glanced at Becca.

"Where's your father? Is he all right?"

She put a hand on my shoulder and leaned close. "You were both in an accident, Mom."

I struggled to get up, but the nurse held me back. "Where is he? Where's Jacob?"

An alarm went off next to my head, and there was a commotion in the room as a nurse ushered the boys out. The noise leaked into my skull and reverberated off the edges of my brain. Becca was crying and I was shouting, "Where is he? What happened?"

"Marlee," someone said. That voice. *His* voice. Older, younger, I couldn't tell. I closed my eyes. Was it real or imagined? Was I back on the mountain or in reality?

"Marlee, I'm here," Jacob said. "Open your eyes."

A few abrasions and a bandage on his forehead. Five fingers on both hands.

"How do you feel?" he said.

"Come on, honey," the nurse said to Becca, and the two of them exited. The alarms were silent. The room quiet. It was just the two of us.

"I'm okay, I guess." I couldn't help staring into those blue eyes. The crow's-feet were mostly gone and the wrinkled skin and gray hair were as well. But it was the same voice. The same as Jay. I put a hand on his arm and there was more than static electricity that shot through me, just like the hand of the old woman. He must have felt it, too, because he seemed to catch his breath and took my hand.

"I thought we had lost you," he said.

"I thought the same about you. What happened?"

"You were right about taking County Line. I never should have chanced it. It was too slick. A truck broadsided us. Your side took the brunt."

"I remember the truck. But then I woke up and you weren't there. I got out of the car and tried to find you. And then I tripped over a rock . . . but it wasn't a rock . . . "

His brow furrowed, he leaned closer and spoke gently. "It's mixed up in your head. The truck driver came back for us. He pulled me out, but you were wedged into your seat. The paramedics had to get you out. And it took them a while just to get there. Do you remember any of it?"

I looked at the bedspread and the IV in my arm. "It was so real."

"What was?"

"The snow. I climbed up a hillside to this house — it was a retreat center. There was an old man inside, waiting for me."

He smiled and took my hand. "No, I'm sorry, Marlee.

You never left the car on your own—you had help from the paramedics and a stretcher."

"Jacob, something has happened. I don't think I can fully explain it, but it's like I've been given a gift."

"Same here," he said with more compassion than usual. "Just having you awake on Christmas is a present for the kids. For all of us."

"We didn't sign the papers, did we? We never made it to the lawyer, right?"

"No. But he still has everything ready. What? Why are you giving me that look?"

"I have a question. Remember the marriage conference we went to a while ago? The one at the church."

He named the speaker and the title of the weekend.

"That's it. They had a conference notebook. Do you remember it?"

"Marlee, you need to rest."

I sat up. "No, this is important. Stay with me. There was a conference notebook; we were supposed to take notes, write some things in there. Do you remember it?"

He nodded.

"You wrote something down during one of the sessions. Just one thing. What was it?"

"That was years ago."

"Jacob, what did you write?"

He looked outside and then at his feet. He rubbed his hands and then looked at me with those blue eyes. "It was something the speaker said. 'Marriage is worth fighting for.'"

Silence between us. He sat in the chair and I searched his face.

"I know we agreed the divorce would be the best thing for us and the kids," I said. "But I'm wondering if we could give it one more try?"

His eyebrows went up and lines formed on his forehead, which he winced through, as he sat on the chair beside the bed. "You really did get knocked in the head."

"It's called a *percussion*." I smiled. "You think I'm crazy, don't you?"

"No, it's just such a change. Like a Green Bay fan rooting for the Bears all of a sudden."

"Something strange happened to me last night. I need to sort it out in my head and then I'll tell you about it."

He patted my hand. "Sure. We can do that. What about the apartment I've rented? What about me moving out?"

"I don't think you should. Unless you want to. Unless you feel like you can't stay any longer."

He glanced out the window and I looked too, at the snow, swirling in the wind of a Christmas morning. The sun cast a golden glow off the surface of the white blanket that covered everything.

"You want to know the truth?" he said. "Having you back with us, after watching the ambulance take you away and not knowing what was wrong — not knowing if you were okay or if you were going to make it — made me do some thinking of my own."

I searched his eyes and in that moment saw Jay, his older, mature self. "Thinking about what?"

"Us. Me. The things I've done to retreat from you." His chest sank a little. "You know . . . the dance we do to keep the distance. To cut out communication and sharing our lives. So much of the time we focus on the kids and what it might do to them." He paused. "But I have to tell you, I know my life won't be the same if we split up."

I sat up quickly, too quickly, and nearly pulled out the IV. "Let me ask you this."

"Careful, you're going to hurt yourself."

"If you could change one little thing about our family,

not a big, huge change, just one small thing, one small regret, what would it be?"

Jacob wrapped both hands around mine and lowered his head, tucking it between his outstretched arms. "There are so many."

"Just one. What was the first thing that came to your mind?"

"It's probably the pet thing the kids talk about. I'd let them have a dog."

I sat back with my head on the pillow, closed my eyes, and a tear leaked out.

"What? Did I say something wrong?"

I shook my head. "No. That was a wonderful answer. Really . . . wonderful."

"What about you?" he said.

"I have a million regrets," I said. "I've never told you how much I appreciate how hard you work for us . . . I don't thank you for providing. Most of the time I'm just crabbing about your hours." I sighed. "Or maybe it's how I look at you. I see your faults instead of the real you — who you're becoming . . . I always thought you were the one who needed to change and then I'd be happy. For the first time I'm able to see myself."

He looked shocked. "Wow. That's a lot better than letting the kids have a dog."

I laughed. "No. It's just the truth."

His expression turned grim. "To be honest though, it's been a long, cold season for us. I don't have a lot of hope."

"That's okay," I heard myself say. "You can hold on to mine."

I looked into the eyes of the man I had begun the journey with so long ago; the mistakes, the choices, the life lived over twenty years.

"I've been thinking about the future." I took a deep breath. "And I think it looks better with us together."

"Even with my driving?"

"Yeah. And I'm glad you took the shortcut. We might have made it to the lawyer if you hadn't."

"Maybe one day you'll regret that."

"I don't think so."

He held my gaze and that warm feeling coursed through me, enveloping me. "All right. Then let's try to work together. Let's make something good happen."

The kids were at the door.

"I think we already did," I said, staring at the cowlick

in David's hair. "We just need to fight. Not with each other, but to stay together. Do whatever it takes."

"It may take some time."

"We have time. And I've learned a good fire can do wonders."

Jacob slid into the bed beside me. One by one the kids ran through the door and hopped up on the foot of the bed.

Outside the snow fell harder. Choices descending like grace. The scene felt like a beginning. Imperfect people unwrapping the perfect gift. It was here I learned there is no barren place on earth that love cannot grow a garden.

Not even your heart.

Afterword

"When do we tell the children?"

As a marriage counselor, those six words grab my heart. I hope they grab yours as well. Couples are making decisions every day that may not seem as momentous as divorce, but like the snow coming down, our choices move us closer to each other or further apart.

I tell couples in the counseling office to hold on to the hope I have for them. I tell couples who come to my marriage retreats that divorce is not necessarily the answer. Some think that divorce will solve all their problems and remove the pain, but often it only compounds the problems and makes things even more complicated. The best chance for a lasting, lifelong love is to work with the person to whom you said "I do." But I realize that isn't easy. I know. I've been there.

In the early years of my own marriage, I cried out to God. Why had He put me with a woman who was so different? So wrong about so many things. Karolyn and I have been married now for fifty years. Those first few years were really rough, but I can see now that they prepared me for what I'm doing today. My wife and I have a rich relationship that has been forged over time and trouble. I'm glad we didn't give up.

No matter where you are in your relationships—single, married, or divorced—my hope is that this story will reinforce the message that there is great power in small choices. There is great hope in a heart turned toward another person. And ultimately, the greatest hope comes from a love outside of us, the love of God who wants to reconcile us to Himself. He was willing to send His only Son on a rescue mission. That's what we celebrate at Christmas. Our prayer is that the hope of His coming will provide hope for your relationships.

One person cannot change another. If you are married to an intractable Jacob or Marlee, your choices can't force them to be the person you want them to be. In fact, who you want them to be may not be the person you really want. But when you choose to change the way you interact with your spouse, it automatically changes the chemistry of the relationship. It's another snowflake in the pot of boiling water. Add more choices to that mix and your spouse has to deal with a difference in the relationship. That person has to deal with another who is showing love to them.

I don't promise happiness for everyone. But I do promise that a devoted spouse who moves toward that other person in the marriage will be much better for those good choices. Many have found the principles in the "purple book" mentioned briefly in stanza 2 of this story to be helpful in this process. The title of the book is *The Five Love Languages: The Secret to Love That Lasts*. Since 1992, it has helped transform thousands of relationships.

I'm hoping Jacob and Marlee read the book and discover their love languages and how to speak that love to each other in a meaningful way. I hope you experience the same.

—*Dr. Gary Chapman*

Discussion Questions

1. List a few of the problems Jacob and Marlee have in their marriage. Which of these problems do you identify with the most?

2. As Marlee views her life in the past, she sees scenes she obviously didn't remember or had pushed out of her mind. Is it easier for you to remember the negatives or the positives from your marriage? Why?

3. Marlee asked Jacob to name one regret. If you could choose one regret from your life that you could change right now, what would it be?

4. Though only Becca knows about the impending divorce, how are the children reacting to the pain in the household?

5. Proverbs 13:12 says, "Hope deferred makes the heart sick." How important is *hope* to a relationship? Do you think you can hold onto someone else's hope for your own marriage?

6. Marlee notices something about Jacob at a marriage conference they attended. She hadn't seen this before. How does this speak to you?

7. In the end, Marlee was not trying to recapture her youthful passion for Jacob, but a new vision of what *might be*. How could a vision like this change your relationships?

8. Two futures were presented for Marlee and Jacob. Which do you think they chose? Did the futures work out exactly as depicted in the story? Why or why not?

9. In the prologue of the novella, Marlee talks about those who feel like they married the wrong person, or that love was frozen over time. What kind of hope from your own life or from the Bible would you give a person who feels this way?

10. In the old woman, Marlee sees someone who knows much more about herself, the Bible, and God than she does. What does this tell you about the path toward a deeper marriage relationship?

11. Marlee also said, "There is no barren place on earth that love cannot grow a garden. Not even your heart." Do you believe this is true? Why or why not?

12. Jesus came to open the eyes of the blind, both physically and spiritually. This story shows the power of "seeing." Is there anything you have seen anew about your life through this story?

THANK YOU FOR READING A MARRIAGE CAROL
Now add your voice to the buzz

visit
AMarriageCarol.com

- Post a review on Amazon.com, ChristianBook.com, BarnesandNoble.com

- Write a review on your blog

- Join the Moody fiction community at MoodyFiction.blogspot.com

- Like Moody Fiction on Facebook

- Follow Moody Fiction on Twitter

MOODY
PUBLISHERS

moodypublishers.com

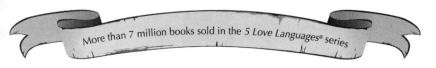
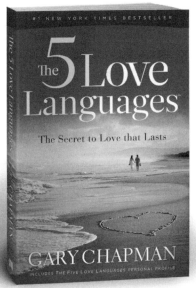